Rainbow
Blob

Butterfly
Blob

Royal
Blue

Ghostly
White

Piggy
Pink

Princess
Powder
Blue

Primrose
Yellow

Mousy
Brown

Grumbly
Green

Poppy
Red

Inky
Black

Grubby
Grey

Giant
Blob

Fizzy
Orange

Canary
Yellow

Puppy
Purple

The Blobs are bright little blobs of
paint which come out of a magic
paintbox into the wonderful world of
Paintbox Land . . .

Grumbly Green
in
Hats Off For Grumbly

The grumbliest Blob in Paintbox Land was Grumbly Green.

Today he was feeling extra grumbly, because the sun was beating down and he didn't have a sunhat. He went to Fizzy Orange's hat shop to buy one.

Now, as you can see, Grumbly's head was an odd shape, a very odd shape indeed. It was sort of long and pointy. The first hat he tried was too small. The second was too tight. It was so tight he thought he would never get it off.

"I don't like where
   I'm going
I don't like where I've
   been.
I'm moany, groany,
   leave-me-aloney
Mumbly, Grumbly
   Green!" sang
Grumbly angrily.

"Here you are, sir. This is a much bigger hat," said Fizzy, dropping a huge cowboy hat on Grumbly's head. But the hat covered more than Grumbly's head — it covered *all* of him!

"This is much too big. I can't see where I'm going and I can't see where I've been!" grumbled Grumbly.

"No problem. Let me help you," said Fizzy. He pulled the hat off so suddenly that Grumbly hit the ground with a *thwack* and an *oof!*

Grumbly tried on lots of hats.

There were small hats and tall hats, round hats and square hats, flat caps and sailor hats. In fact, he tried on every hat in Fizzy's shop but nothing fitted! Grumbly's head was just the wrong shape for hats. It was far too pointy.

Grumbly left the shop and walked along all moany and groany. The sun got hotter — and Grumbly got hotter — and hotter. Then he saw a marvellous sight — a row of traffic cones. "Hats!" said Grumbly. "Hats! And they're all my size!"

He picked one up and popped it on his head.

But as soon as Grumbly put the traffic cone on,
Constable Blue, the police Blob arrived.

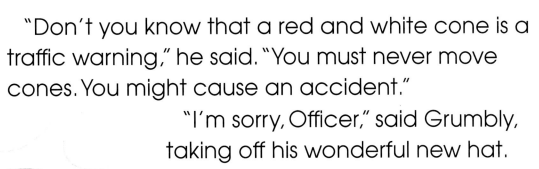

"Don't you know that a red and white cone is a traffic warning," he said. "You must never move cones. You might cause an accident."

"I'm sorry, Officer," said Grumbly, taking off his wonderful new hat.

Grumbly walked through the park. Then — vroom,
vroom! Along came a witch on a broom. It was Inky Black.
"What's the matter, Grumbly?" she called.

"I need a sunhat," said Grumbly.

"Broomsticks and bats. Try one of my hats," said Inky.

"Thank you, Inky. You're not as black as they paint you after all," said Grumbly, as the witch's hat dropped on to his head.

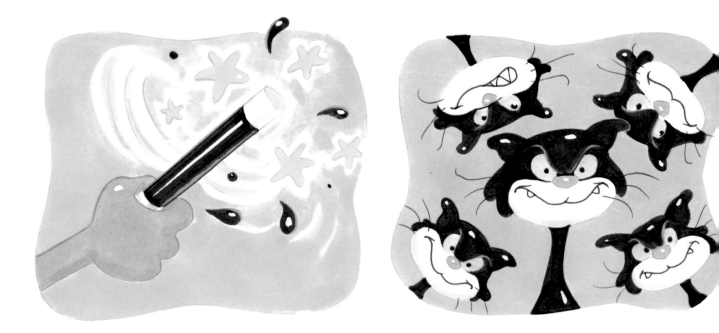

But Inky wasn't being kind. She was being mischievous! She pulled out her magic wand and waved it.

"While Grumbly wears my witch's hat, he'll be chased by black blob cats," she chanted.

In a flash, five black cats appeared and began to run after Grumbly.

"Oh, no," he grumbled. "They all think I'm a witch. Go away! Leave me alone!"

But the cats chased Grumbly uphill, down dale and all over Paintbox Land.

Grumbly had to get rid of his lovely new hat just to get rid of the pesky cats. The cats were very disappointed.

"Oh, no! He isn't a witch after all!" one miaowed. "He was just pretending. What a swizz. Typical!"

Grumbly thought he was the unluckiest Blob in the whole of Paintbox Land. But he wasn't. Floury White the baker was much more unlucky.

As Grumbly passed the baker's shop there was a loud bang and clouds of flour blew out of the shop.

This was followed by a shower of nuts and bolts.

Then some springs came bouncing out of the doorway and off down the street, boing, boing, boing!

"Ooh, whatever is going on?" cried Grumbly as a spring bounced past him. "That nearly hit me on the nose — or was it my toes? I could have been hurt. Who's being so careless with their springs and things?"

Grumbly peered into the shop. Floury White was
sitting on the floor looking dazed.

"I'm Floury the baker
I'm white from toe to top
From making bread and pizza
In my floury baker's shop," sang Floury sadly.

"What's up Floury?" asked Grumbly. "Are you all right?"

"No, I'm not," replied Floury, rubbing his head. "My doughnut machine is broken."

He led Grumbly into the bakery, where huge piles of doughnuts reached up to the roof.

"What a disaster!" cried Grumbly.

"It is," agreed Floury. He looked at Grumbly. Then he looked at the doughnuts. Then he looked at Grumbly again.

"Wait a minute," said Floury. "Your pointed head could help."

"Are you sure?" asked Grumbly. "Pointed heads are no good for anything — especially hats."

But Grumbly was wrong. His pointed head was perfect for making the holes in doughnuts.

Soon every doughnut had a hole.
"Thanks, Grumbly," said Floury. "Is there anything I can do for you?"

"You don't happen to have a spare hat, do you?" asked Grumbly. "One that would fit a pointy head?"

"No I don't, but I might be able to help you just the same," said Floury.

The baker chose three doughnuts from the pile.

"Alley oop, alley oop, alley oop," cried Floury as he threw the doughnuts on to Grumbly's head.

They made a perfect hat.

"Thank you, Floury," said Grumbly.

For once Grumbly wasn't grumbling. In fact he was grinning from ear to ear.

Grumbly was so happy with his new sunhat. He danced and skipped and skipped and danced until he was tired and hot — and *hungry!*

But that was no problem. He had a snack on hand — or rather on his head!

And Grumbly's special hat was delicious.

"Yum, yum. Yum, yum," he said as he munched the doughnuts one by one.

And Grumbly wasn't grumbly anymore, because he knew he could always buy another hat at Floury White's bakery tomorrow!